VAMPIRE HEARTS WEREWOLF EYES

A Shadow Queen Novella

Eva Peony

Copyright © 2022 Eva Peony

All rights reserved

The characters and events portrayed in this book are fictitious. Any similarity to real persons, living or dead, is coincidental and not intended by the author.

No part of this book may be reproduced, or stored in a retrieval system, or transmitted in any form or by any means, electronic, mechanical, photocopying, recording, or otherwise, without express written permission of the publisher.

ISBN-13: 9798497088427

Cover design by: Art Painter
Library of Congress Control Number: 2018675309
Printed in the United States of America

To All Who Continue To Read,

Thank you.

CHAPTER ONE

Everyone believes that Vampires are gone, but not me. They are not cowards that get easily scared. After all, I do not think they have lived this long by being scared. I think of how things used to be before they came, but nothing comes because they have always been there. In the shadows, always there but never seen, if not harming us then protecting us, but they're still there. That is why I don't believe they are genuinely and forever gone.

"Meredith!" My mother shouts from her room.

"Yes," I do not look at her; instead, I look at the changes that she has made. The bed is pushed to the side, clothes scattered on the floor, and the vanity is lined with a variation of lipsticks, eyeliners, and spilled nail polish.

"What do you think?" She asks with an eager smile on her face; only now do I remember that she is going out. My mother is still looking at me with that eager smile.

I tell her what she wants to hear, "You look lovely," I

say, pretending to care; after all, I do not like her new boyfriend. So, it really doesn't matter what I think; that was made quite clear to me a very long time ago. "Don't wait up; I'll be home late," she says, heading down the stairs at the sound of John's car in the driveway.

"Ok," is all I say, hoping she leaves soon, so I can go back to my room and drown in my sorrows.

Once sure they won't come back, I walk up the stairs and lock myself in the sanctuary that I've created for myself. I look out the window past the cemetery and the forest to the loneliness. It is midwinter, so there isn't much snow sticking to the ground. The children play with each other while their parents talk; nothing really changes. I love the loneliness; it's all I have.

Not wanting to look anymore, I go to sleep and dream the same dream. One of a wickedly handsome Prince holding me in a pool of stars. The next day I wake up to the sound of my mother ravaging through the kitchen cupboards. I go down the stairs to find pots and pans scattered over the floor.

I take the last step and ask, "What are you looking for?"

"Oh, did I wake you?" she asks as if meaning it. Last night's makeup smeared.

"No," I lie; truth be told, I was having a great dream until I heard her awful noise. There was a hauntingly beautiful Prince.

Mother looks up from her rummaging, "Have you seen the silverware? Your Grandmother is coming."

Grandmother, I don't think I've seen either in a very long time, "Top shelf left corner. Which Grandmother?"

"Annabel, your father's mother," She says this with little care, for I have never known my father, only his family. Now that I think about it, I haven't seen my Grandmother since I was ten, either one actually. Truth is, I didn't even remember we had any relatives alive.

For a very long time, it's just been the two of us, that is not counting mother's various paramours, "Oh, I'm going to get ready for school," I head back upstairs and throw myself on the bed. Another year and nothing changes; at least now I can take off. Will, what I've saved be enough?

With great effort, I push myself up and head for the bathroom. No use pondering such things now.

"Don't be late. Your Grandmother isn't a patient woman. After all, she came because it's your eighteenth birthday. Don't make her wait," mother shouts as I head out the door.

"I won't. Don't worry!" I start down the stairs and onto the paved road. Perhaps I should leave tonight; if I can find the place of my dreams, would I even need a high school diploma.

Salvador joins me in step; something about him makes him seem all too alluring yet at the same time makes my skin crawl. I've only spoken to him once, and that was when I was eight. Now that I look at him, I find his aura has darkened. For whatever reason, I feel as if he were a predator stalking his prey, and it has nothing to do with what he is.

Salvador tilts his head to the side, charcoal black hair falling into his eyes, "Hi, Meredith," his voice has a calmness that doesn't match his eyes.

Tucking a strand of crimson hair, I say, "Hey," and dig my nails into my palms. Why is he joining in step with me? What the hell does this guy want?

He clears his throat before saying, "Happy birthday." Why does he know that? I've never celebrated a birthday, let alone mentioned it to Raven. "Thanks," I say, uncertain if I should question him or not.

"What are your plans for tonight?" he asks.

Looking forward, I say, "Same as always," why should I elaborate.

From my peripheral vision, I can see him struggling with something. He reaches for me but drops his hand at the last minute.

"Is there something you need from me?" I ask as we approach the gray building surrounded by potheads and stuck-up hags.

Raven rushes towards us, "Mer!" her musical voice so out of place with our surroundings.

I lift a brow at her, "Raven, how are you today?" my tone's a bit bitter but then again, who told her to go around telling people it's my birthday.

"Hey, what's wrong?" She looks between Salvador and me. "You said you wouldn't tell."

"I didn't; you did. I'll see you around Meredith," Salvador heads towards his friends who linger by the old oak tree. Luke's eyes remain on me a little too long for my taste.

"Ok, so sue me, it just came up," she says as Ignacio takes Leo's book bag and throws it to Scar. Something tells me after tonight, those two will be no more.

"Really, and since when do you talk to him?" I ask as we walk off the cemented walkway and onto the gravel path that leads to the entry stairway.

Raven gives me a warm smile while wrapping her arms around me, "Don't be mad, he's in my Spanish class, and I needed help with my homework, at some point, it came up," even she doesn't believe that lie.

"Who do you think you're fooling?" I ask, breaking free of her hold and entering the building. Raven hurries after me and throws her math book into her locker.

I continue on my way to Miss Mel's class as we take our seats; Becky pulls out her mirror and lipstick; I swear she's more cosmetic than human. Raven gives Becky an odd look as the blond fixes her hair into a ponytail. When we were children, Becky and Raven were best of friends, and then one day they weren't. Raven refuses to talk about what changed between them.

Becky pretends to fix her bra strap, getting the attention of some of the guys. She gives them a smile she probably thinks is attractive before tossing her ponytail over one shoulder. If only she knew what they say about her behind her back.

As we wait for class to start, Raven leans over, "what are you doing for your birthday?"

"Why, so you can broadcast it to the entire school?" I

ask.

Raven lowers her head as if aware I can see the lies in her eyes. But knowing how she can't keep a secret, I've never told her what I am nor what I can do. Before Raven can speak, Miss Mel walks in ever so pleasant the grumpy hag frows at everyone. No one told her to piss off the gods how she envies our youth. Miss Mel wears her gray hair in a tight bun, making her narrow face look stretched out and out of place. Her voice sounds like an ogre with a toed stuck in its throat.

The guy next to me leans over, "Hi, I'm Antonio," he extends his hand in greeting. He was with Luke and Salvador earlier how did he get here so quickly?

I ignore his extended hand and instead look over to the Valkyrie sitting by the window. It seems everyone is coming out to play today.

"I don't know why she sent you," I say, looking into Antonio's lupine eyes, "but I'm not interested."

If I had to guess, I'd say this is Annabel's doing. While my mother remains under her control, I play at being mortal. Since I play at being mortal, Annabel will probably try to make her grand reveal tonight.

Holly turns her attention to me, her hazel blue eyes looking into my soul as they shift colors revealing that she has had a premonition. Since I met her, she has always told me what these premonitions mean. Without looking down, Holly scribbles something onto a piece of paper and slips it onto my desk.

Once Miss Mel turns to write on the blackboard, I

open the paper, "don't trust them." it reads. Then as the premonition came, the writing goes, fading now that the message has been delivered.

Miss Mel makes a throat-clearing sound that makes me think of one of those gargoyles from the movies that make a screeching sound as it's about to attack. She looks over the class with scrutinizing eyes as she opens a book with her skeletal hands; from what I can see, the book is about the Fallen. I don't mean the fallen angels; I mean the immortals.

As Miss Mel is about to start her lecture, the intercom makes a crinkling sound before a voice is heard urging students to head to the auditorium immediately.

Someone whispers, "do you think it has to do with the body they found in the gymnasium?"

"I heard it was laid out as if in sacrifice," someone else says.

"What body?" Antonio asks.

"This morning, they found a girl covered in strange markings, dead," Carina says, "and she didn't even go to our school."

"How do you know this?" I ask as we make our way towards the auditorium.

"Sabrina's dad is the groundskeeper," Carina says, "he came in the early morning and found it. Cops showed up and cleaned everything up like nothing happened."

"Did the wind not tell you?" Holly asks, her eyes looking slightly glazed.

"No, Holly," I wrap an arm around her and pull her

towards the bathroom. Raven is oblivious to my absence. "Did the wind speak to you?" I ask once I'm sure we're alone.

"Last night, they whispered, but it wasn't clear until this morning," Holly holds on to my arm, "you can't let them take me." She tightens her hold on my arm, "if they do, I'll never come back."

"Who wants to take you away?" I ask.

Holly starts to shake, so I wrap her in a hug and start to pet her head. When we were five, I found her curled up into a ball by a hollowed-out oak. The rest of the kids in our class had picked on her for being different. Holly's mother made it no secret she believes in the occult, and the children driven by their parents' fears decided to stone her to death.

Of course, the school turned a blind eye until I knocked out the principal's son. Then they acted like the world was ending. They had called mother in, but she was no help. On the other hand, Holly's mom threatens to sue the school for discrimination and abuse. James never bothered either one of us again. Granted, what happened to him after school may have been the real reason, he never bothered anyone again. Everyone thought he'd gone mad.

Since that day, whenever frightened, Holly comes to me. Even now, they ostracize her as if she would give them the plague.

"The men in white," Holly finally calms down enough to speak, "they will blame this on me."

"Why?" Even though the reason is irrelevant, I ask, a scapegoat is always needed and better than the town

Seer.

She looks up, tears streaking her pretty face, "you know why."

Indeed, I do, "are they here?"

She nods, her heartbeat rising, "it's alright, I'll get you out," I let go of her and take the hoody I keep in my bag out, "wear this, will leave campus while everyone's distracted."

Holly obeys as I peek my head out; the hallway still has a few straddlers. I wait until security is chasing them down the hall to bring Holly out. We barely make it to one of the emergency exits used by the staff to go out and have a smoke.

Mr. Silver leans against the worn brick wall, eyes closed. "I would hurry if I were you," he says without opening his eyes. Mr. Silver is a fox spirit and one of the two immortal teachers at the school, "hide her where no one can find her." He tosses a small pouch my way before putting out his cigar and heading back into the building.

There is only one place I can think of to take Holly, and that is to a biker bar at the edge of town; no one messes with them. Since Holly's mother is no more the only people looking for her will want to hurt her. We get as far as the edge of the woods before our path is blocked by Salvador.

"I don't know where you think you're taking her," he says, all pretense is gone, "the Order wants her."

"I don't give a rat's ass what the Order wants," I say, letting my eyes flash, showing him just a hint of what lies beneath my skin.

"You already know what you are," he says as a wave of darkness knocks him out. I don't need to look up to know that blast of dark wind came from the crow. Ever since I meet the beautiful stranger the crow has been with me; I feel this crow is somehow connected to him.

We make it out of the woods and onto the road as the bus leading out of town approaches. Lucky for us, the bus is practically empty, a mother and child being the only passengers. When we near the bar's stop, the drive hesitates before letting us off.

A burly-looking fellow stands by the blood-red door, a bottle of beer in one hand and a cigar in the other. He snorts but lets us through the last time I was here; I almost took Luca's eye out; I do wonder if he still remembers.

I guess he remembers; a dagger flies towards me. I dodge it with ease, spinning Holly out of the way. I raise my hands, "let's call a truce," I smile at the Wolf King.

CHAPTER TWO

L uca snarls as he takes the dagger out of the wall, "why should I?"

I give him my most charming smile as I say, "because the bitch is back and she wants the Seer," walking over to him, I trace a finger down his delicate jaw, "I highly doubt you want her getting her hands on a Seer of all things."

Holly freezes in place as all eyes turn to her, "don't worry, the bastard won't hurt you," I say, pulling the girl towards the bar, "sit."

Luca gives Niko instructions before we head into his office.

"Why is she here now?" Luca takes a seat behind his desk.

"Apparently, to make her grand reveal," I say, "unfortunately, as I was bringing Holly to you, one of her mutts realized I'm already aware of what I am or at least what they think I am."

Luca leans back in his seat, eyes closed; he lets out a sigh, "why now off all times?"

"Also, a girl was killed "cops" covered it up," I walk over to the bar in the corner and pour myself a glass of honeysuckle wine, "the Order wants Holly; odds are they make it seems like it was her doing."

"Do you know who it was?" Luca looks even more haggard than when I first met him.

"The victim no, all I've heard is she wasn't even a student at my school she was, however, killed in ritual style," I take a sip of wine, "as to who did it, well I don't believe in coincidences Annabel's always had her people in place could be her doing."

Luca opens his eyes as I set my glass down; we rush out of his office to find Holly trying to claw out her own eyes.

"What the fuck happened?" I take Holly's arms and twist them onto her back before sinking my fangs in. The Vampire bite can lull one's prey into a state of ease, something Holly clearly needs.

"One minute she's rambling on about death and deceit; the next she's trying to claw her eyes out," Niko looks at me with a tinge of fear in his eyes, "she said you would burn the world down."

"Sometimes what she sees has a double meaning," I lift Holly up, "where should I place her?"

"Hand her to Celest," Luca instruct, "take her to Mother Hanna; perhaps she can help her control her visions."

Celest takes Holly, Niko at their heels.

"What did she see?" Luca asks once we're back in his office.

I take a gulp of wine and collapse onto his leather

couch, "something that shouldn't be possible," I say as I pinch the bridge of my nose, "I think Annabel wants to breach into other worlds and rule them all."

"What did she see?" Luca repeats.

"A dead world, chaos, ashes, blood," I laugh, "I rose from the ashes and burnt it all down."

Luca studies me for some time before saying, "fuck."

"That's all you have to say?" I ask with a tad bit more amusement than intended, "are you not going to preach about how killing me when you found me could have prevented all of this."

Luca shakes his head, "if I'd killed you, then that bastard would have my head."

"Who?" I ask as a familiar touch of darkness caress my spine.

"You'll find out soon enough," Luca says, "just head home for now."

"Holly."

"We'll take care of her," he says, "I'll have Arthur take you home; try to act surprised when you see her."

I snort, "like that would change anything," I pat the old King on the shoulder, not expecting him to take my hand and pull me towards him, "tell no one what she saw," Luca commands as he lets go, "good luck kid."

"Thanks," I head out, not paying much mind to the curious looks I get from the rest of his pack. I find Arthur in the same place as before, leaning against the door; he's the only bear in Luca's pack, their cousins or something of that sort.

"Everything alright little doll?" Arthur asks as he

pulls up to the house; I call home.
"Thanks, big guy," I say before; hopping out of his
truck, I head home.

CHAPTER THREE

The house has a coldness to it. I've only felt once before, "Meredith, do you have any idea of what time it is?" my mother asks, hands shaking. Her concern for once seems genuine.

Once upon a time, she was actually a loving mother, but then Father died, and she changed, becoming everything Annabel accused her of being.

The stench of fear fills the house, "Not a clue, dear mother. Oh, did I miss her?" I ask sarcastically as I close the door.

"Go to your room!" she shouts, yet her eyes tell me to run.

I make for the stairs catching a glimpse of a hooded figure. Snorting, I stop by the side table next to the stairs and grab the hidden dagger strapped to the bottom. "Tonight just keeps getting better and better," I say in a sing-song voice, "either help or get out," I say to no one in particular.

"Meredith," mother's voice is pleading, "just go to your room."

Slipping the dagger into my sleeve, I turn, "but you see, mother, I have developed the sudden need for blood."

The figure emerges from the kitchen gun aimed at my head. That wretched stench I've smelt before.

"Mother, you truly need to select better partners," I sidestep in time to avoid the bullet. Why must guns be so loud?

A shadow-like figure swoops into the room, taking my mother out of the house. He really came; I guess Fay really keep their word.

"Abominations must be exterminated," John shouts as he tries to reshoot me.

I tsk, "if I'm an abomination, then what are you?"

The shadow figure appears behind John, snapping his neck with little to no effort. Then incinerating him in dark flames.

"You should be more careful," the Prince says, "you nicked yourself with that dagger I gave you."

I smile at the lovely Prince, "had I been careful, you wouldn't be here," I bow my head placing my free hand over my heart, "thank you," he is the loveliest creature I have ever laid my eyes upon.

The Prince gives me a wolves grin, "we are even now. If you were to need something else in the future, a new bargain would be struck."

I take a step towards him, then another, how I wish to run my fingers through his midnight black hair, to trace the shape of his ears to burrow my face in his firm chest. But to him, I am only a child, and it can never be a Prince from another world another time not even in my dreams can I be with him.

"It wasn't meant to be," he says, probably reading my thoughts, "it'll only cause you heartbreak."

"What if I have no heart to break?" I ask foolishly.

The Prince catches one of my tears, "and yet I can hear it beat." He places a hand over my brow, "I can take it all away."

I step back not because I fear him but rather because forgetting would truly kill me. As if understanding, he nods and instead pulls out an obsidian ring.

"For old times' sake," he takes my right hand and places the ring on my pointer finger. I can feel the cool stone merging with me, "if you are ever at death's door, just call out to me."

Out of fear that more tears will fall, I only nod. The night my father died, I met a Prince sent to our world to complete his Accession. Due to a war he had been in before entering our world, he was half dead when I found him, and I was no better. I pulled out the obsidian arrow from his chest, and in turn, he healed my wounds. After I was found, I left him food until he adjusted to our world. Before he left it, the Prince ensured I knew how to survive.

With only the stars and moon as a witness in the cover of night, he showed me how to fight, hunt, and run. Then he left, promising to return if I ever needed him. He left me an obsidian dagger, the only proof he was real and that I wasn't insane.

The Prince kisses my forehead before dissipating into shadows. I fall to my knees' tears streaming down my face. Why couldn't he just take me with him? Why does it hurt so much? I've crawled into a ball when they find me.

Mother keeps apologizing, but I can't even bring myself to say it's not her fault. The pain I feel I've felt before, and it won't ever go away. Annabel shows up at some point, but I do not care. Why is she even here?

"This is all your fault," Annabel yells at mother as I'm lifted up, "if she had left with me when she was a child, she wouldn't be like this."

Something within me finally snaps, "how can it be her fault," I snarl, breaking free of Salvador's hold, "when you are the reason Father is dead."

Annabel looks at me as if unable to believe anyone would dare go against her, let alone accuse her of anything.

"Take her upstairs," she commands, "lock her in her room until I'm done."

I move in time to nock her of her feet, "No!" I stand before her and my mother, "for all I know, you went inside her head and made her what you wanted," my lip curls back, "I was there that night; I saw how you executed your own son to save your skin."

Annabel lets out a manic laugh, "be grateful you are the last of my bloodline," she tries to stand, "what have you done?" confusion overtakes her as the poison spreads. After all, how could she know about the dagger hidden in my sleeve? The dagger is laced with poisons that have no effect on me.

I take a step towards her, "Your reign is over," I say, kneeling on one knee, "I know all your sins. I have always known what I am and who I am. I can assure you, we are not Kin," I bite my lip, "father knew all you wanted was our blood; it's your curse. A vampire who can only feed off her descendants. It's quite fucked up if you ask me."

Annabel attempts to sneer, but it seems she's lost all strength.

"What do you mean?" Luke asks.

"My father learned what his dear mother was up to," I don't look away from her as I speak, "when father confronted her, she killed him. Annabel is not a true Vampire; her bloodline is far more diluted than ours."

"Did she kill my mother?" Luke asks.

"Odds are yes," I stand and lift Annabel up, tossing her onto the couch, "you could go into her head and find out."

Luke seems to debate this for some time, "she made me hurt you," he says, "I wouldn't put it past her; if she killed your father, then she must have gotten rid of mother."

Blood starts to seep out of every poor in Annabel's body, eyes and mouth until her skin turns to ash, "Should I or do you want to do the honors?" I ask Luke.

He looks from Annabel to me, "she owes you more than she does me."

"That's up for debate," I walk to Annabel and plunge the obsidian dagger into her chest. Nothing but ash and blood remains.

CHAPTER FOUR

L uke agrees to help clean out John's place while Antonio spreads a rumor that John went back to the city. Salvador seems to be the only one reluctant to believe Annabel was anything other than his savior. Perhaps this is why he was so easily blinded by her.

John's place is practically deserted if not for the dead demon hounds at my feet and the newspaper clippings you'd think no has lived here in a very long time.

The clippings all date back to 1996 and stop at 2001. There are newspaper clippings about the four of us. At least one, if not both, parents dying Luke getting kidnapped after his mother's death. While I supposedly got lost, the police found me three days later covered in blood. Why in the world did John keep tabs on us of all people. He even wrote how none were natural accidents but rather cover-ups by E. Who the hell is E?

None of this makes any sense; were John not dead,

I'd kill him all over again.

"What should we do with all of this?" Luke asks.

"Get rid of it," I say, "on the other hand, pack it up. I want to study it some more."

"So, you give the orders now?" Salvador leans against the entrance to John's bedroom.

Something about him doesn't seem quite right, but I don't have time for this, "if you are not here to help, then get out." I walk past him.

"You were wrong," Salvador says, "about Annabel."

"You weren't there," is all I say. There's no use arguing when it's clear he's been brainwashed by Annabel.

Mother sits cross-legged on the worn sofa, a cup of steaming coffee cradled in her hands. She looks younger than she has in years, yet at the same time, Mother seems as if she carried the weight of the world.

I toss my bag next to the old rocking chair, "What is it?"

Mother takes a deep breath before blurting out, "we're moving in with your grandparents."

"Grandparents?" I take a seat in the rocking chair and start tapping my fingers against its arms.

She bites her lower lip, "my parents," ma takes a few gulps of coffee, "I think it's best we stay with them."

"You've never mentioned them before," in truth, I always assumed mother was an orphan.

"That's a complicated story," Ama avoids looking me in the eye as she adds, "they'll be happy to meet you."

So, that's what she's up to, "You want me to go live with them; am I such a burden you need to be rid of?" I rise, sending the rocking chair flying back. The sound of wood colliding against the wall is enough to tell me the thing is beyond repair.

Mother sets her cup down ever so delicately, "they're the better choice."

"Look at me!" I stride forward, pick up the cup and toss it behind me, porcelain colliding with glass. "Why do you hate me so much? What did I ever do? Last night I figured the reason you changed overnight was due to what Annabel did to you, but now I'm not so sure that's the case."

She looks up, eyes rimmed with tears and hatred, "I thought I could love you, but I can't; every time I look at you, I'm reminded of him and all the things he put me through."

"If you hated him so much, why did you have me?" I lower my head, so we're eye to eye, "why did you hesitate that night? Had you killed me as you planned, you wouldn't have to look at my abhorred face every day for the past eighteen years."

"Meredith!" Mother raises her forehead bumping into mine.

I let out a mocking laugh, "Elizabeth! You have some nerve raising your voice at me when you haven't even earned the right to be called my mother."

I catch the scent of a wolf, and something else as a voice says, "Regardless, she is still your mother."

I let my lip curl as I turn to find a middle-aged female standing at the doorway, "and who the hell are you?"

CHAPTER FIVE

The female shakes her head, disappointment in her eyes, "you've done a magnificent job at raising her."

With a snort, I say, "but she didn't raise me; I raised myself." I run my tongue over my fangs pressing the flesh against one until I can taste blood, "I'm eighteen now; by law, I am legally an adult. I'm not going with you, and you can't make me."

"Like you can control what you are," the female retorts, "I'm not your mother; do not think your temper tantrums will work with me."

"Listen, old lady, you clearly did a crappy job at raising her," I don't even look at Elizabeth as I add, "or else she wouldn't be so fucked up." I step towards the newcomer when a male appears behind the tiny female. His eyes are an odd mixture of green and brown with tinges of blue and gold; they complement his dark skin beautifully.

"I take it I have you to thank for my height and full lips," I say, earning a smile from the male I presume to be my Grandfather.

He nods, his dreadlocks catching in the sun, "you wear gold in your hair?" I move the tiny female to the side to get a better look.

"A mortal wouldn't be able to see that," his voice has a rumble to it that makes me think of dragons or thunder, "but then again, you're not mortal."

"I never was," I say, taking a step back, "I'm not going with you."

"You need to learn control," he says.

"I have not the thirst for blood nor the damned need to turn under a full moon," I say, "I learned to control it long ago."

His smile reaches his eyes as he says, "but you're one more thing, my dear child."

Crossing my arms, I ask, "and what would that be?"

With that same smile, he says, "Dragonian."

"I'm what?"

"A Dragon," my Grandfather adds, "my father came from another world; for whatever reason, the gene skipped your mother. We figured that since your Grandmother is a wolf and I am a dragon, the two canceled out, making your mother mortal, but you, my child, prove that is not the case. I can feel the flame coursing through you."

I turn to look at Elizabeth, "You really can't shift?"

"Not once in my lifetime," she says, "that's why your father mistook me for Mortal. I don't even smell like a hound."

"Mere...

Luke and Antonio stand behind my Grandfather,

boxes held high.

"We can come back?" Luke takes a step back.

Before they can run away, I say, "Stop!" They flinch but obey, "bring them in."

They do as told and set the boxes where the rocking chair used to be.

"We're gonna go now," Antonio takes a step back, then stops as if uncertain about his next move.

"That would be a waste of time, boy," Grandfather's voice rumbles a warning or perhaps a threat.

"He's a dragon; you're a hound," I say, "you don't stand a chance."

Antonio straightens while Luke holds back a laugh, "I can take him."

"Not that I doubt you," I say, patting his shoulder, "but something tells me he's far more ancient than he seems and thus has had more time to learn how to snap you in half."

"She's not wrong about that," my Grandmother chimes in.

"Wait, he's a what?" Luke points at my Grandfather.

"Dragon," I wave him away, "so do you live in the world Great-Grandfather came from?"

"I've never set foot," Grandfather says, "my father had no way of going back until my mother passed."

"Why?" The question has a double meaning that only I know.

"To enter his world, permission is required from the powers that be," Grandfather places a hand on my shoulder, "he'll visit soon; perhaps you'll have better luck than my mother did. But for that, you'll have to come with us."

I look from him to my mother, Grandmother, Luke, and Antonio, trying to figure out if this is all a dream; I ask, "How do I know you're not lying?"

"Fay can't lie," Grandfather says.

"Dragons are Fay?" I ask.

"A type of Fay," he says.

Remembering what the Prince taught me, I say, "but they can bend the truth."

Grandmother laughs, "who told you that?" her eyes seem to search for something.

Meeting her gaze, I say, "I read it in a book."

Grandfather sighs, "having the two of you under the same roof will be like old times, I'm afraid."

"What?" we ask, causing him to flinch.

"Nothing, pack whatever you need," with that, he steps out of the house, taking with him all the warmth. With the lack of his presence, the living room suddenly seems bigger.

"Where are you going?" Antonio asks.

"She's trying to get rid of me," I say, walking past Elizabeth. If what Grandfather said is true and Great-grandfather visits perhaps, I can go to their world and look for the Prince. Granted, I have no idea if they're from the same world. It's still worth a shot.

CHAPTER SIX

Packing doesn't really take long; most of my belongings are already packed in my emergency bag. I just drag, because why not? The emergency bag contains money I've earned working odd jobs here and there, along with potions the Prince taught me how to make an extra pair of shoes and some clothes. I pull out a second duffle and toss a few books along with my blanket and a few hoodies.

Biting my lower lip, I power on the burner phone Luca gave me and text him I'm leaving town. Take care of Holly; Annabel is no more.

Luca: Take care, call when you have a chance.

M: Will do.

Grandmother stands at the foot of the stair's eyes scrutinizing my every movement. Ignoring her, I head for the door. Luke and Antonio are nowhere in sight.

"Won't you say goodbye to your mother?" Grandmother asks.

I don't even bother stopping as I say, "I have no mother."

Grandfather sits inside a blue pickup engine already running. He hops down and takes my bags, tossing them in the back; he covers them with a tarp, "it's been raining in Chicago," he motions for me to climb in.

I open the door and ask, "You live in the city?"

"Yup," he says, "don't worry, the neighborhood we're in is warded, so shifting is safe."

"Wait for us!" Antonio shouts as Luke beats him to the truck.

"We wanna go," Luke says.

"You left to pack?" I pick up a fallen sock.

"Yeah," Antonio takes the sock and shoves it into his duffle, "this place sucks."

I think I blink more times than normal because Luke pats me on the shoulder and says, "It'll be alright besides nothing fun ever happens in this damned town."

"You agreed to this?" I look at my Grandfather, who just shrugs.

"Could you use some hands at the restaurant," Grandfather climbs into the driver's seat just as Grandmother makes her way down the pavement.

She scrunches her nose as she asks, "What's this?"

Before I can answer, hooded figures descend upon the property surrounding us on all ends. Considering all that's been happening. I stupidly let my guard down, and now we're surrounded by the Elite.

CHAPTER SEVEN

"**I**'m afraid we can't let you go," one of the hooded figures steps forward, "so if you would be so kind as to come with us."

I reach into my pocket and press the one on the burner phone, "I have no business with the Elite," I say, hoping Luca's picked up. The Elite are worse than the Order; they believe only pure bloodlines should exist. The narcists even named themselves the Elite.

"If you're waiting for the mongrel and his beast to come to your aid," a female voice says, "I'm afraid you'll be waiting a long time."

"Will I know?" I shrug my hoodie off my skin, feeling like it's on fire, "What makes you think a bunch of inbreed cunts can take on Luca and his pack?"

I've only used the flame twice in my life; he was with me both times. I let flames of shadow, flames of darkness, and bitter delight rise from my toes to my head. The flame seems to accept me this time.

"You never said she was an abomination," the male

that spoke first says.

"We can save her," Salvador steps forward, "please Meredith, let us save you; we can be together like before."

I let out a manic laugh as memories of my previous lives flood my mind, "do you truly believe in each lifetime I was with you by choice," I continue to laugh, "did you ever wonder why I never bound my soul to yours?" I send out a ring of flame and watch with amusement as it consumes the female that mocked Luca, "Fool all of you fools. Thinking you could trap me here, how mistaken you are."

So many wish to come out and play, "what bring the Damned here today?" I ask.

"We have come to collect a promise," the one that speaks has a jagged scar running down his left eye over his nose and down to his throat, Anole.

"And what promise is that?" I ask.

"Meredith," Elizabeth's voice is barely a whisper. One of the Elite holds her, a gun pressed against her temple.

"Truly pathetic what kind of immortal uses a gun?" Without moving a hand, the gun starts to overheat until the bastard is forced to drop it, and just in time as it implodes on its self.

"She cannot be saved," someone says.

"Who asked you to save me," I say, turning my attention on the head of the Elite, "sure as hell wasn't me." Opting for a gorier approach, I use the wind to my advantage and let it hide my steps as I appear behind the leader of the Elite, reach into his chest cavity, and rip out his heart, engulfing it in flame as I crush it with my bare hands.

"Now, what is it that I owe?" the Damned don't seem faced by what I've done, but my Grandmother looks at me as if I were a walking nightmare.

"Meredith," Grandfather calls out, "you need to loosen your hold on the flame and let it go back to dormancy."

"But I don't want to," when I look at Grandfather, I find he's engulfed in golden flame, nothing like my dark one, "you can't all truly believe light is good and dark is evil, can you? Because in case you weren't aware, dark and light are just metaphors created by the man to divide us."

"I have to say I most definitely agree with that sentiment," a voice that makes my insides turn on each other drawls.

"I see," I say, addressing Leila, "that wretched being remains; alright, I'll deal with it for you. But in your next life, you and your brother must serve me for eternity."

The Damned are Vampires turned by Enrique, the narcissist of all narcissists and my once lover. Honestly, what was I thinking, but being with him wasn't my choice either. These cursed fools insist on trying to trap me here. Too bad for them, I won't let them.

CHAPTER EIGHT

Enrique smiles at me as if we were true lovers, "how I've missed you, my Irina," he reached a crocked hand out. It seems he never recovered from our last fight. How many lifetimes must I live before I can be rid of them?

"That name's quite old," I say, "I never cared for it." So long as the flames engulf me, he won't approach after all; that's how the skin on his chest got scarred.

"What's happened to you?" Raven's sing-song voice asks.

I extinguish the flames now that all players are here, let's see who gets to die first. As the flame returns to dormancy, I pretend to collapse. Not surprisingly, Raven rushes over, feigning concern; she reaches in, trying to absorb what isn't hers to take.

"You couldn't help but follow me into this reincarnation as well, could you?" I ask, shoving the crystal Mr. Silver gave me into her chest. "I strip you of immortality. May your descendant curse you for all eternity Zariah, you have no one to blame but yourself," I say as her face contorts in pain, "well, I suppose you could blame the Celestial Lord for allowing you this idiotic task."

"Silvia," Enrique reaches out.

"Not my name either," I place my foot on Raven's throat as I stand, "no matter what, you were all promised today is the night you die."

Holly wasn't wrong; I would burn this world down along with all who inhabit this plane of existence. I'm tired of having to pay for loving who I want. What's so great about being a deity when there are only restrictions.

"You never put it to sleep," Grandfather's eyes are filled with horror, "what have you done?"

"This world will end," I say with a smile as my flame reaches the core of the earth connecting with it. I start to pull it towards me, I will set us free we will be together, and the rest of the Deities be damned if they get in my way.

###

A voice calls out to me somewhere deep within my mind, pulling me to the surface. It seems it's not just my spirit that gets to leave this place. I hold on to that voice to that hand and let it guide me back to the surface. I let it lead me to my other half, my soul becoming one as I rise from the ashes of a now-dead world.

And there amongst the ashes, he waits in all his glory clad in darkness; the Deity of the Underworld takes me into his embrace, "welcome back, my Empress."

COMING LATE

2022

READ ON AHEAD

ONCE BITTEN
TWICE TURNED

CHAPTER ONE

The sound of the music reverberates from my toes to my head, sending an electrifying shiver down my spine. It has been two years since the world turned chaotic, two years since I last saw a band live, two years since anything truly made sense.

Everyone just works as if that were all that can be done. I'm sick of working, sick of having to rush home to make curfew of having to spend whatever time remains a slave to the system.

Ma believes it'll get better; I say it'll only worsen.

Someone taps my shoulder. The acrid stench of cigarette smoke clings to the stranger. The smell amplified the moment he leaned down to whisper in my ear, "wanna go have some fun?" the stranger's raspy voice made me think of a dog with a bad cough.

I take a step back, bumping my back against someone's shoulder, "Sorry, not interested," I say, turning to apologize to the person I bump into. A girl with cat-like eyes smiles at me, but she hisses when the stranger tries to reach for me. The man's eyes widen, uncertainty filling his slightly glossed-over eyes.

"Who sent you?" the girl asks, but the stranger doesn't get to answer as he starts to convulse.

The girl lets out a sigh before taking my hand and pulling through the crowd. "You don't want to be caught," she says as the sea of people part for us. Someone notices the convulsing man. Next thing you know, everyone is trying to get out.

Concerts, like most things, are currently forbidden; the Enforcers will show up soon and lock everyone up. We make it outside just in time to duck into an alley the bands already loaded up.

"You two want a lift?" the drummer asks.

"I'm good," I say, breaking free of the girl's hold, "thanks."

"To him or me?" the girl asks.

"Both," I walk past the band's van and duck into a separate alley. Having decided I no longer care if I live or die. I've taken it upon myself to learn the city's ins and outs, like all the shortcuts and even the entrance to the Forgotten City.

As I'm about to make the final turn, something pulls me back, sharp pain spreading from my throat to my heart. Something like claws digs into my abdomen and shoulder, my vision blurs as my knees go weak. The last thing I remember is the taste of something metallic flooding my mouth and dripping down my throat.

###

Something nips at my shoulder while something

else digs into my ribs. I open my eyes to the loveliest moon I have ever seen. The moonlight calls to me, pulling me towards her I somehow climb out of the ditch I'm in. Where am I? I topple over my foot, catching on a root.

When I reach down, the pain in my ribs intensifies. I reach back and pull out two wooden daggers. Something runs through the shrubbery before I can question how I got here, triggering something within.

I close my eyes and inhale, my senses overwhelmed by the sound of wolves howling, of songbirds and owls hooting. Most importantly, by the beating hearts and pulsing blood, I track the tiny creature and, without hesitation, sink my fangs in. Warm blood pools in my mouth; I don't stop until the little creature stops fighting.

Something is watching me, but I do not care; the hunger consumes me. I need more. Following the sound of sleeping hearts, I stumble upon a farm. Without a second thought, I drain the cattle, the chickens, the pigs. Even the farmer that got in my way. Would it be wrong for me to say I feel no remorse?

With my hunger sated, I head back into the forest; those eyes continue to follow my every move. But I do not care; perhaps I'll have dessert. Footsteps, no paw steps near me, and as I turn, something knocks me to the ground. Warm fur graces my fingers tips.

I try to throw the wolf of me, but somehow, he's more powerful. The wolf sinks his canines into my shoulders. Causing me to let out a growl of disapproval. Before my eyes, I watch as the wolf trans-forms into a man. His golden-brown eyes burn with a question, "Who are you?" and a command "stay down."

"Well, this is interesting," a female voice says, "it seems there was no saving you."

There is a familiarity to her when the male climbs of me. I look up to emerald cat eyes. The male takes the jeans and boots; she hands him.

"I'm Mika," she extends her hand towards me, "what's your name?"

"Lilith," I say, surprised at the change in my voice, "What am I?"

"Vamp," the male growls out, "a reckless one at that."

"Don't mind, Sean," Mika says, "he dislikes every-thing and everyone."

Standing I dust myself off, Sean's bite seems to have given me a sense of clarity, "Where am I?" I ask the easier of the two questions. Did I really kill that man?

Sean seems to know what I'm thinking; he takes a step towards me, leaning down, he whispers, "yes."

Something about how he utters that one word has me inching to fight him. How was I supposed to know what I was doing? I raise my hand, but he catches it midway, "Be careful little vamp, or tonight might be your last night."

Mika steps between us, forcing Sean to let go; he shakes his head as he walks away midnight hair swaying in the moonlight. "Don't mind my brother; he lacks certain sensors."

Brother, I look from Mika to Sean while there is a resemblance. I can't help but say, "but you're a cat."

Sean sneers while Mika giggles, "our mother has a thing for shifters and the such, we also have a brother that's a lion and one that's a crow. Actually, I'm more of a yokai, to be precise a bakeneko."

"I don't know what that means," I say.

Mika smiles as she starts to guide me towards her brother, "I'm not surprised," she says, "our myths, much like yours, are rarely explored."

Mika leads me towards a black SUV while Sean trails behind us, a Crow rest atop the roof; he flaps his wings and flies towards us. Shifting as he lands, a hauntingly beautiful Male stands before me. His eyes remind me of amethyst encased in silver like Sean and Mika; his hair is midnight black. His skin is only slightly fairer than Sean's. At the sight of his brooding brother Crow snickers.

"What's the matter," Crow twirls a strand of my muddy hair, "brother, the two of you just met, don't tell me you already plan on claiming her."

"You think I'm some Fay bastard that…

Before Sean can finish his sentence, a roar cut's him off.

Mika leads me around her brothers and into the SUV, "Try growing up with three insufferable bastards," she shuts the door behind me and climbs into the driver's seat. Sean takes shotgun, and Crow settles beside me.

"That roar?" I ask as something taps my shoulder. I turn to find a lion curled up in the back, his paw resting on my shoulder, "you weren't kidding."

Mika laughs while the lion pats my shoulder. Crow snickers as I watch with amazement as yet again, someone transforms before me. A golden light emanates from the lion, and then there's only a sleepy-looking Male.

"I'm Leo," he extends his hand towards me, "mom has a sense of humor," Leo adds, at my confusion.

I turn to Crow and ask, "So then are you, Crow?"

He responds by laughing, "you can call me whatever you want," he leans in, and flick's my chin.

"Rafael!" While soft, Mika's voice holds enough command to get Crow to sit back on his side of the truck, "ignore them all."

The rest of the drive passes by in silence until a thought hit's me, "how did I end up in that ditch?"

"The Vamp that turned you shouldn't have been hunting in your city," Leo says, "wannabe hunters caught up to him. After he got away, they took you out of the city; the wooden daggers didn't go in deep enough to kill you."

"You know all this, how?" I ask as anger rises.

"Rafael was able to track you through your energy imprint," Mika says, "it's been four days; your family believes you dead. For them and for yourself, it's best if it remains that way."

"Four days," I say more to myself, "wait, why were you tracking me?"

Sean looks at me through the rear-view mirror, "Mika made us; she can sense when somethings off."

Even if she can sense when something is off, what's

it to her? "That's all you're going to say?"

"What else would there be?" Sean sneers; it seems that his favorite expression.

"Ama might be able to help you," Mika says.

"As long as you haven't had mortal blood, you should be fine," Leo adds. At my frightened look, he leans in, sniffing my throat, "oh, you're screwed."

ABOUT THE AUTHOR

Eva Peony

Chicago Native Eva when not writing can be found reading and binge-watching K- dramas & C-dramas.

BOOKS BY THIS AUTHOR

Between Shadows & Darkness

Red Snow

Once Bitten Twice Turned

Coming Late 2022

Embracing Darkness

Coming 2023

Book Three in the Shadow Queen Series

Bittersweet

Ongoing E-Novel find it on KindellVella

www.ingramcontent.com/pod-product-compliance
Lightning Source LLC
Chambersburg PA
CBHW030411160726

47992CB00007B/3074